SanD HaSSLe

by Howie Dewin
Story by Amy Keating Rogers
Based on
"THE POWERPUFF GIRLS,"
as created by Craig McCracken

SCHOLASTIC INC.

New York   Toronto   London   Auckland   Sydney
Mexico City   New Delhi   Hong Kong   Buenos Aires

ISBN 0-439-25059-5

Designed by Peter Koblish

Illustrated by Alex Maher

12 11 10 9 8 7 6 5 4 3   1 2 3 4 5 6/0

Printed in the U.S.A.
First Scholastic printing, August 2001

SUGAR . . .

SPICE . . .

AND EVERYTHING NICE . . .

These were the ingredients chosen to

create the perfect little girl.

But Professor Utonium accidentally

added an extra ingredient to

the concoction —

CHEMICAL X!

And thus, The Powerpuff Girls were born!

Using their ultra superpowers,

BLOSSOM,

BUBBLES,

and **BUTTERCUP**

have dedicated their lives to fighting crime

and the forces of evil!

Chapter 1

The city of Townsville, where our super-heroes, The Powerpuff Girls, have been work-ing round the clock to rid their fair city of monsters, Mojo, and mayhem . . .

WHAM! Buttercup flew straight into one of the eyes of a bright purple five-headed monster.

BAM! Blossom followed up with an un-dercut punch that made the monster's tongue stick out. Then she doubled back

1

and came at the monster, ready to deliver a superkick to its belly.

KA-POW! Bubbles finished him off with a final extra-powerful zap of her eye beams.

The monster crumpled into a ball on the ground and slithered away as quickly as it could.

"Chalk up one more victory for the good guys!" Blossom declared. But the

excitement in her voice sounded forced. She was very tired.

"Yippee," muttered Buttercup. She was so tired she was actually drooping as she flew. It looked like she might fall asleep in midair.

"Is anyone else as worn out as me?" Bubbles asked wearily.

"I'm toast," offered Buttercup.

"Then I'm burnt toast," grumbled Blossom. "It's been nonstop for weeks."

"Well, I'm flying nonstop right to bed," said Buttercup. The three Girls headed slowly back to their home in the suburb of Pokey Oaks.

Half asleep, they flew slowly toward

their front door. They just had to get a few more feet —

"GIRLS!" The front door burst open and there stood Professor Utonium, exploding with energy. He had a huge smile on his face.

The Girls hung in the air, sagging from the weight of being awake.

"Hi, Professor," they yawned.

"Have I got some great news for you Girls!" the Professor exclaimed.

"Can we hear it later?" asked Bubbles sleepily.

"We just need to" — Blossom interrupted herself with a yawn — "take a little nap."

"We're a little beat," Buttercup explained, trying to slip past the Professor and up the stairs.

"But that's the good news, Girls!" The Professor was not giving up. "I just got off the phone with the Mayor. He agreed that you Girls have been working too hard. He's given you all clearance to take a little time off!"

The Girls opened their sleepy eyes in surprise.

"So, tomorrow morning, we're off to the beach!" The Professor spread his arms open wide.

The Girls were silent for a moment. Then they began to perk up.

"Really?" squeaked Bubbles.

"Like a real vacation?" asked Buttercup.

"You're a lifesaver, Professor!" cried Blossom. She threw her arms around his neck.

Suddenly the Girls were zooming through the living room. They slalomed up the stairs. They slid down the banister.

"Ya-hoo!" they screamed. Then they hurried up to their bedroom. Only they weren't headed for bed anymore. They needed to pack their bags!

Chapter 2

It's a perfect Townsville day. The sun is shining, the birds are singing, and The Powerpuff Girls are on their way to a little rest and relaxation. . . .

Nobody wasted a single second in the morning. Buttercup ate her breakfast with her goggles and flippers already on! Blossom and Bubbles were all decked out in their brand-new sunglasses and bathing suits.

Faster than you can say "fun in the sun," the Girls were in the car and ready to go. The Professor came out wearing a sporty outfit of his own, balancing all their suitcases. Soon they were on their way.

As the Professor and the Girls drove along they could smell the salt air. They knew they were almost to Townsville Beach.

"It's a beautiful, sunny, perfect beach-ball day," Bubbles sang.

"This is so awesome," crowed Buttercup as she watched some older kids on their surfboards. "I'm gonna swim and roller-skate and find a good volleyball game!"

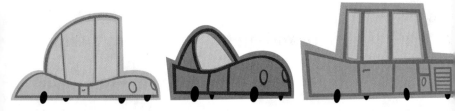

"Not me. I'm going to ex-pand my seashell collec-tion!" Blossom announced.

"I am going to build the most beautiful sand cas-tle that has ever ex-isted," Bubbles said happily. "And then I will fill it with bunnies."

"Whatever!" said Buttercup, rolling her eyes. "Wow, check out the surf!"

"Just remember, Girls, we only have the weekend and I want you all to relax and get some rest in between all your fun," cautioned the Professor.

"Professor," said Blossom, "we are su-perheroes! We are not just good at fight-ing crime, we're also very good at being on vacation."

"That's right!" agreed Buttercup. "I bet we can have at least twice as much fun as normal people."

"Well," said the Professor as he pulled the car into a parking spot, "let the games begin!"

The Girls spilled out of the car and tore down to the beach. They found a perfect spot in the sand and threw down their towels and toys. Bubbles immediately

went to work on an amazing sand castle for her bunnies.

Blossom wasted no time at all. She strolled along the water's edge, looking for colorful additions to her shell collection. Her first find was a beautiful pink shell with a fossil imprint.

"Hey, Professor!" she shouted. "I just found a very rare scientific artifact!"

The Professor smiled and waved at his brainy charge.

Buttercup was in the water in an instant. She struck up a conversation with a young boy on a surfboard. In no time at all, Buttercup and her new friend were taking turns on his surfboard and her sea horse float.

It truly was a perfect day, even better than they'd imagined. Townsville and crime-fighting seemed a million miles away.

"Okay, Girls, who wants something from the snack bar?" The Professor stood up by the blanket, wearing his old swimming trunks and a wide-brimmed hat. Blossom had to bite her tongue not to giggle. The Professor looked so funny!

"I'll take a hot dog," she began. But before she could finish her order, a scream filled the air.

Blossom and Bubbles spun around toward the water. People were running out of the ocean as fast as they could. They were grabbing up their children and running toward the parking lot.

"What's happening?" Bubbles asked.

"I don't know," Blossom said as she strained to see past the people and out into the water.

Buttercup zoomed over to her sisters. "Can you believe this?" She seemed very annoyed.

"Believe what?" Blossom answered.

"Believe that!" Buttercup pointed across the beach and out into the water. Blossom followed the direction of her sister's arm.

There, just past the sandbar, was a family of enormous sea monsters.

"Oh, dear," sighed the Professor.

The monsters were headed for the beach. There were four of them. And

even the two kid monsters towered above the people of Townsville. They must have been fifteen feet tall!

"They had to choose this beach and they had to choose today?" Buttercup said in disbelief.

The Girls stared at the monsters. Meanwhile, the tourists of Townsville were getting a little hysterical. As the monsters drew closer to the shore, the citizens' screams and shouts became deafening.

Is this some kind of evil plot? Will The Powerpuff Girls EVER get any rest and relaxation?! Girls! Snap to it! There are monsters to battle!

Chapter 3

Buttercup stared with blank eyes. Blossom just shook her head. Bubbles said in her smallest voice, "But this was supposed to be our vacation. . . ."

"Oh, for pete's sake!" the Professor muttered.

"Of all the beaches in all the world and they had to step onto this one," Buttercup said in disgust.

"Look out!" Blossom shouted. The panicked crowd was coming right at them as they fled the monsters. It was a stampede! The Girls grabbed their things and zipped out of the way.

"Yikes!" squeaked Bubbles.

"They're more dangerous than the monsters," said Blossom.

"Excuse me!" snapped Buttercup as she dove to save her inflatable sea horse from being trampled.

"Guess we better get in there, Girls," Blossom finally said, taking the lead.

Bubbles stood up. "Okay, I'm ready," she said in a very un-excited voice.

Buttercup put down her snorkel and prepared to battle, even though for once, she didn't want to. But then the Girls heard a strange noise. It started as a low rumble that gradually grew louder and louder. Before long, it was clear that it was people's voices.

At first, the Girls couldn't tell what the people were saying. But then they saw a small group of cranky citizens marching back toward the water. They looked really mad. They were chanting, "Take Back the Beach! Take Back the Beach!"

As the Girls watched, more and more people joined the marchers. Pretty soon, it was an angry mob.

"Monsters Not Allowed! Monsters Not Allowed!" Another group started a different chant.

"Human Beings! Fight for Your Rights!" People seemed to be coming from all directions now. They were chanting and heading straight to where the monsters were standing. It looked like the citizens of Townsville had finally had enough. They were tired of monsters spoiling all their fun.

"Wow!" Blossom said. "It looks like the citizens of Townsville are doing it for themselves. Girls, maybe we can continue our vacation after all."

"Sounds good to me," Buttercup declared.

"Yeah, me too," Bubbles agreed.

But as The Powerpuff Girls watched, they could tell something wasn't quite right. The people of

Townsville weren't just rallying to protect themselves. They seemed downright mad and vengeful! Their faces were red and angry and contorted with hatred. The air was filled with hysterical screams.

Blossom gazed at the citizens thoughtfully. Then she switched her focus to the monster family. They stood in sharp contrast to the raging hordes around them. They looked shy and almost scared! Even

though they towered above the crowd — the humongous mom, the gigantic dad, and the two enormous kids — they seemed totally unprepared to defend themselves.

But that didn't seem to matter to the mob on the beach. The citizens of Townsville were starting to attack the monsters! Hundreds of people were kicking up sand and throwing shells.

As the shells hit the monsters, they lifted their overgrown arms and tails to protect themselves. The papa monster's arm swung through the air to block the shells from hitting his son. In the process, his arm accidentally swiped several citizens, sending them flying through the air.

It was an innocent move by the monster dad, but that's not how the people of

Townsville saw it. Now they were all the more convinced that they had to destroy these monsters! One of the angriest citizens called for the police. Another called the fire department.

Before The Powerpuff Girls had made a single move, even the army was on the way!

"Girls," said Blossom slowly as she stared at the monsters, "does something about this seem strange to you?"

Her sisters were gazing at the monsters. Suddenly, they understood what Blossom was talking about. They had to stop the citizens of Townsville from making a terrible mistake.

What? The Powerpuff Girls are going to turn on their own friends and neighbors? Have they been tricked? Is this some kind of joke? Girls! What are you thinking?

Chapter 4

"Take that!" shouted the ringleader as he hurled driftwood and rocks at the monster family. The other citizens followed his lead.

The monster family actually looked frightened. The parents tried to protect their children, but the little monsters just stood there, stunned.

"I'm the last one to want to interrupt our vacation, Girls," said the Professor, "but don't you think you ought to do something?"

"Look at the little one," said Bubbles, pointing her arm at the littlest monster who stood fifteen feet tall. It looked like it might cry. It had its feet in the edge of the water, and it was hanging on to a bag of sand toys.

"Wow," Bubbles added, "imagine the

castle I could build with those sand molds!" The molds were as huge as the monster family.

"That monster looks really scared," Blossom remarked. "I think it's just a baby."

The Professor seemed to be getting a little nervous. "But it's a monster."

"The older one looks a little frightened, too." Buttercup pointed to the bigger of the two kid monsters. It stood holding a snorkel and goggles and flippers. "You know, except for the fact that it's about fifteen feet tall, that kid really looks just like us. . . ."

"I know," said Blossom. "That's what worries me." But before she could say anything else, the Girls heard a familiar voice.

"Blossom! Bubbles! Buttercup! Do

something! You have to help! I know you're on vacation, but this is chaos! You have to save us, Girls!" It was the Mayor. He was stumbling as he tried to run across the sand. He looked a little silly in his usual suit coat and hat on a

beach full of people in bathing suits.

"Why are you just standing there?!" he asked.

"I've been wondering the same thing, Mayor," the Professor agreed.

"Excuse me, Professor, Mayor," said Blossom, "but you both need to take a deep breath and calm yourselves. I don't think we're in as much trouble as you think."

"Wha — but — how . . . " the Mayor

sputtered. He looked at Blossom like she had lost her mind. "They're huge! They'll destroy us!"

The Professor nodded in agreement, his eyes large with fear.

"They have sand toys and snorkels," Buttercup responded.

"We think they're just here to have a nice vacation like the rest of us, Mayor," Bubbles piped up. "By the way, look at my sand castle! Isn't it beautiful? It's for bunnies."

"It's lovely, Bubbles, but I'm afraid you Girls have gone soft on me. Look at the panic! Look at the confusion! Monsters are attacking! How can you say they aren't dangerous?"

"It's the citizens of Townsville that are creating the panic, Mayor," Blossom said wisely. "In fact, it's hard to tell who the real monsters here are!"

"It's the citizens who are the mean ones!" declared Bubbles.

"Hmmm," said the Professor as he looked over the scene. He was reconsidering the situation. "You Girls may be right."

"Well — well — well . . ." the Mayor sputtered. But before he could say anything

more, a group of attacking citizens ran past. They completely trampled a little beach cabana and the lifeguard station, just because it was standing in their path.

The Mayor threw his arms up in the air and turned to The Powerpuff Girls. "I don't care what you do, Girls, but DO SOMETHING!"

If the citizens of Townsville are hysterical, and the Mayor is hysterical, and even the Professor has his doubts — how do we know the Girls are right? What if they're wrong? Is this the end of Townsville?

Chapter 5

"Okay, Girls!" shouted Blossom. "Back me up!"

The Girls leaped into the air, with Blossom in the lead. She swooped down next to a lifeguard and grabbed the bullhorn right out of his hands. The lifeguard was shocked.

Bubbles and Buttercup zoomed off to catch up with Blossom, who was now perched atop the lifeguard's very tall chair.

31

"Ladies and gentlemen of Townsville," Blossom's voice boomed out of the bull-horn. But no one seemed to be listening.

"Hey!" Buttercup grabbed hold of a man who was rushing by. "Listen up, buddy! My sister's talkin'!"

But it didn't seem to do any good.

"People! Listen to me!" Blossom shouted. "Please stop! We beg you! We believe these monsters have come in peace, in the name of good, old-fash-ioned family fun!"

It was as if she wasn't even speaking. The people below continued to run around madly and throw whatever they could find at the monster family.

"Blossom!" Buttercup was shouting for her sister. "Take a look at that!"

The Girls turned their attention to a

huge red fire truck that had pulled onto the beach. The truck's hoses had already been unwound, and it looked like the firemen were just moments away from blasting the innocent monster family with a huge jet of water.

"We gotta deflect the water, Girls!" Blossom was already in the air. Bubbles and Buttercup swooped down along the water's edge and grabbed three surfboards that had been left behind by hysterical kids.

Without a second to spare, the Girls got themselves into position. No sooner had they lifted the surfboards into the air than they were bombarded by powerful spouts of water. The

boards deflected the water and shot it straight up into the sky, creating a huge water fountain that rained down on the whole beach.

From below, the confused and frightened monsters looked on with some relief. It was clear that The Powerpuff Girls had just saved them from being blown halfway across the ocean. But that was clear to the people of Townsville, also, and they were none too pleased!

"Hold the line!" Blossom shouted as they struggled to keep the boards in place. "I'll go shut off the water supply."

"Hurry!" Buttercup shouted back, nodding toward a line of police cars. "We've got more trouble on the way!"

The police were gearing up to bombard the monsters with smoke bombs. The Girls had to stop them. But they couldn't move till Blossom got the water shut off. The huge spray of water finally sputtered out. The Girls shot across the sky just in time to block the first round of smoke bombs. Without a second to spare, they started batting away the missiles like they were playing volleyball — except in this game, there were dozens of balls! One by one, Blossom, Bubbles, and Buttercup swung at the smoke bombs and sent them far out over the ocean, where they fell into the water and fizzled out.

The monsters continued to watch the Girls with a mixture of confusion and relief on their faces. The citizens of Townsville, however, were even more furious. They were beginning to throw their rocks and sticks at The Powerpuff Girls!

Then a voice rang out from the crowd below. It was the same voice that had begun the attack on the monsters in the first place.

"Get The Powerpuff Girls!" the ringleader's voice cried out. "They're working for the monsters!"

"We can't attack The Powerpuff Girls!" another voice argued.

"But they're *helping* the monsters!" the original voice shouted.

"Maybe they're not really The Powerpuff Girls! Maybe they're imposters!" shouted another voice. An angry roar rose up from the crowd.

Blossom, Bubbles, and Buttercup looked at one another in dismay.

"What do we do now?" Buttercup shouted.

Uh-oh. It looks like the people of Townsville are turning monstrous on the Girls!

chapter 6

Before The Powerpuff Girls had even a moment to figure out their next move, a small group of very angry citizens stepped out from the crowd. The Girls zoomed down to the beach in hopes of negotiating with the crazy mob.

But there was no time for talk. The troublemakers had a pile of rocks and sticks at their feet. They even had a few smoke bombs that they'd gotten from the police.

And they were getting ready to throw them right at Blossom, Bubbles, and Buttercup!

As the rocks and sticks started sailing through the air, the Girls shot back up into the sky while they tried to make a plan.

"This is nuts!" cried Buttercup. "These people have really and truly turned into monsters. I think it's time to kick some Townsville butt!"

"We can't do that," argued Bubbles. "These are our friends and neighbors."

"With friends like that, who needs enemies!" grumbled Buttercup.

"Bubbles is right," declared Blossom. "We have to defend ourselves, and we need to protect the monsters, but we don't want to hurt these people. They're just confused and *temporarily* monstrous. They're not really bad people."

"Okay, then what do you suggest we do?" Buttercup snapped. Just then, a big rock whizzed by her head. "Holy mackerel! They've built a giant slingshot!"

Below them, the troublemakers had finally gotten organized. They were getting ready to pummel the Girls with all their ammunition.

"I need to talk to the people," Blossom said thoughtfully. "But I can't do it with that group of troublemakers in the way. We need to take care of them, and then I think we can reason with the rest of the folks."

"Leave it to me," Buttercup declared.

She zipped past her sisters and down toward the beach. She hovered just above the sand and started to spin in a circle, faster and faster. Soon, she was nothing more than a blur. She was like a whirling dervish. Her spinning was acting like a drill in the sand, creating a very large hole.

It didn't take Blossom and Bubbles long to figure out Buttercup's plan. They had to get the furious troublemakers into the

pit. They'd have to trick them into back-
ing in. Once the people had fallen into
that hole, they'd be good and trapped.

Blossom and Bubbles zoomed down to
the troublemakers. They zipped by them
from the right and then from the left. The
Girls got the troublemakers so confused
that they were turning in circles.

The irate people kept trying to fire their
slingshot. But Blossom and Bubbles
didn't stop. The two sisters spun the
people to the right and then to the left,
until everyone was completely dizzy.
Then, when the people were very close to
the edge of Buttercup's giant pit, the Girls
surprised them from behind and got
them to spin around so their backs were
turned toward the hole in the sand. That's
when Blossom and Bubbles started lung-

ing at them, making them back up, step-by-step. And then — *KER-PLOP!*

"WHOA! YIKES! HEY!" The voices of the troublemakers rang out as they fell to the bottom of the pit.

"Watch your step!" shouted Buttercup.

"Nice work, Buttercup!" Blossom called. She was zooming toward the bullhorn again.

There was no time to waste. The Girls had taken care of the troublemakers, but now the rest of the crowd was getting restless. They seemed like they were almost ready to attack the monsters — even *without* the troublemakers leading the way.

It was up to Blossom to make them understand. She flew up to the lifeguard's chair and once again attempted to reason with the citizens of Townsville. She took a deep breath and started to speak.

"Ladies and gentlemen, my fellow citizens of Townsville — my sisters and I are here to ask you one simple thing — STOP! It is time to stop the senseless attack on this innocent (though very large and somewhat scary-looking) monster family.

"My sisters and I believe they come in

peace. We believe they are here simply to soak up a few rays, snorkel in the surf, and build a sand castle or two. Perhaps it is time that we look at the ways in which we are the same instead of just the ways in which we are different. They are a 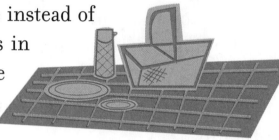 family with two young children. They have beach toys and a picnic basket. They have sunscreen and dark glasses. We have so much in common that I believe we can get along!

"I suggest that this monster family should be as welcome as anybody else on this public beach. After all, they are just here for a little vacation from monstering. They are no different from any of us!"

Blossom let the bullhorn fall from her mouth. She looked at the faces in the crowd. The people seemed to have really listened to her. They seemed to be thinking about what she had said.

From the back of the crowd, the Professor shouted out, "Bravo!" He began to applaud loudly.

Blossom looked at her sisters. Bubbles was cheering. Then she looked at the monster family. It was obvious the monsters were very touched by her speech. The mama monster was even wiping away a tear from her big monster eye.

After a moment of silence, a voice rang out from the crowd. "But how do you know they're just here for a vacation?" shouted the voice.

The rest of the crowd began to mumble.

47

There were many heads nodding in agreement.

"Yeah! How do we know?" This question echoed from every corner of the crowd.

Blossom could tell she had to think fast. The crowd was starting to get angry again.

"Let's ask them!" Blossom answered.

The idea of actually talking to the monsters silenced the crowd. The people of Townsville, along with Blossom, Bubbles, and Buttercup, turned to the monster family. The tension was thick in the air. The citizens stared at the monsters and waited for someone to speak.

"Well?" said a voice from the crowd.

"How about it?" Are you just here for a vacation?"

The monsters stared back at the crowd and didn't say a word.

Uh-oh . . . looks like the monster family is claiming "no comment." You better look out, Blossom! If those monsters are looking for something more than a little R&R you're going to have some explaining to do!

Chapter 7

"Mr. Monster? Mrs. Monster?" Blossom tried to sound confident, but she was starting to get nervous about what the monsters would say.

The monsters didn't say anything. Instead, one of the little monsters looked up at its father. The father looked back at his child. The father nodded to the little monster. The little monster turned back to the crowd. It seemed to be looking for someone. Its eyes came to rest on a little girl standing at the front of the crowd. She was about four years old, and she was holding a pail and shovel.

The little monster stepped away from its family and toward the little girl. The crowd gasped and pulled back. The girl's father grabbed his daughter and held her in his arms.

But the little monster didn't stop. It just

kept waddling toward the crowd until it was standing directly in front of the father and daughter. Then it reached into its bucket of toys and pulled out a star-shaped mold. The little monster held it up to the little girl.

The crowd was overcome by the little monster's generosity. "Awwwww," they cooed together. The sand mold was actually monster-sized and was big enough to crush the little girl, but no one cared. It was the thought that counted, and the people of Townsville seemed very happy with the thought.

"Let's hear it for the monsters!" It wasn't clear who was shouting, but Buttercup was pretty sure the voice sounded like the Professor's.

"Hip-hip-hooray! Hip-hip-hooray!" the crowd roared.

The monsters broke out into big smiles as the people of Townsville lined up to shake their claws. Blossom even heard a few apologies from some of the people as they introduced themselves to the monsters.

"Nice speech," Buttercup whispered to Blossom.

"Thanks," answered Blossom. She smiled as she watched the children on the beach begin to play with the monster kids. Then she and Buttercup

joined Bubbles, who had gathered all the kids together to play.

"Let's work together," declared Bubbles. And she began to show the children how they could build the biggest, grandest, most magical unicorn sand castle that ever was, with a little help from their new friends.

"Friends can come in all shapes and sizes," declared Blossom.

"Yeah," Buttercup agreed. "And in the summer, everything's better in monster size!"

And so once again, the day is saved, thanks to The Powerpuff Girls! And a special thanks to Bubbles for turning this sand hassle into a sand castle!

The action-packed adventures of

BLOSSOM, BUBBLES, AND BUTTERCUP

CARTOON NETWORK

THE POWERPUFF GIRLS ™

Available wherever you buy books, or use this order form.

❏ BFG 0-439-16019-7	Chap. #1: Powerpuff Professor	$3.99 US
❏ BFG 0-439-16020-0	Chap. #2: All Chalked Up	$3.99 US
❏ BFG 0-439-16021-9	Chap. #3: Cartoon Crazy	$3.99 US
❏ BFG 0-439-16022-7	Chap. #4: Blossoming Out	$3.99 US
❏ BFG 0-439-24325-4	Chap. #5: Teacher's Pest	$3.99 US
❏ BFG 0-439-24326-2	Chap. #6: Party Savers	$3.99 US
❏ BFG 0-439-25058-7	Chap. #7: Scary Princess	$3.99 US
❏ BFG 0-439-17305-1	8X8 Mojo Jojo's Rising	$3.50 US
❏ BFG 0-439-17306-X	8X8 Bubble Trouble	$3.50 US
❏ BFG 0-439-16013-8	8X8 Monkey See, Doggy Do	$3.50 US
❏ BFG 0-439-19105-X	8X8 Paste Makes Waste	$3.50 US
❏ BFG 0-439-25055-2	8X8 Snow-off	$3.50 US
❏ BFG 0-439-25179-6	8X8 Beat Your Greens	$3.50 US
❏ BFG 0-439-21036-4	8X8 Bubble Vision	$3.50 US
❏ BFG 0-439-29589-0	8X8 Bought and Scold	$3.50 US

Scholastic Inc., P.O. Box 7502, Jefferson City, MO 65102

Please send me the books I have checked above. I am enclosing $_____ (please add $2.00 to cover shipping and handling). Send check or money order — no cash or C.O.D.s please.

Name _____ Birth Date: _____

Address _____

City_____ State/Zip _____

Please allow four to six weeks for delivery. Offer good in the U.S. only. Sorry, mail orders are not available to residents of Canada. Prices subject to change.   PPG801

www.scholastic.com/titles/powerpuffgirls

SCHOLASTIC